SUPER SAURUS
SAVES KINDERGARTEN

Written by
Deborah Underwood

Illustrated by
Ned Young

Disney • HYPERION

Los Angeles   New York

Printed in Malaysia

First Edition, June 2017

1 3 5 7 9 10 8 6 4 2

FAC-029191-17125

Library of Congress Cataloging-in-Publication Data

Names: Underwood, Deborah. | Young, Ned, illustrator.
Title: Super Saurus saves kindergarten / by Deborah Underwood ; illustrated
by Ned Young. Description: Los Angeles ; New York : Disney•HYPERION, [2016] | Summary:
Arnold, who is nervous about his first day of kindergarten, transforms himself into Super Saurus to face what
turns out to be not so frightening, after all. Identifiers: LCCN 2015019319 | ISBN 9781423175681 (hardcover)
Subjects: | CYAC: First day of school—Fiction. | Kindergarten—Fiction. | Imagination—Fiction. Classification:
LCC PZ7.U4193 Sup 2016 | DDC [E]—dc23
LC record available at http://lccn.loc.gov/2015019319

Designed by Tyler Nevins

Text is set in Century 725 Bold/Monotype and CCJScottCampbellLower Italic/Fontspring

Reinforced binding

The art in this book by Ned was created by using acrylics on illustration board. Arnold chose acrylics and colored pencils on watercolor board to create his masterpieces.

Visit www.DisneyBooks.com

For Kenn and Heather
—D.U.

For Hadlee, who loves dinosaurs
—N.Y.

Kindergarten was starting in two days, and Arnold was busy making plans . . .

. . . to escape.

"Why? Kindergarten will be fun," said Emily.

"Ha! What if the teacher is Zorgo the Evil Genius?" asked Arnold.

"The teacher is Mr. Zachary," said Emily.

"What if he feeds kids to his pet T. rex, Krok?" asked Arnold.

"They wouldn't let a teacher have a T. rex," said Emily. "They won't even let us bring pointy scissors."

"No kindergarten in the universe can hold me," said Arnold "Do you know why?"

"I have a guess," said Emily.

"Because," said Arnold, "I am . . ."

Super Saurus packed . . .

and plotted . . .

and packed some more.

The big day arrived. "All ready?" Mom asked.

"Oh, yes," said Arnold.

Super Saurus was taken prisoner inside a submarine.

When the hatch opened, he whooshed away
in his Super Saurus Scuba Suit. But . . .

. . . he was quickly recaptured.

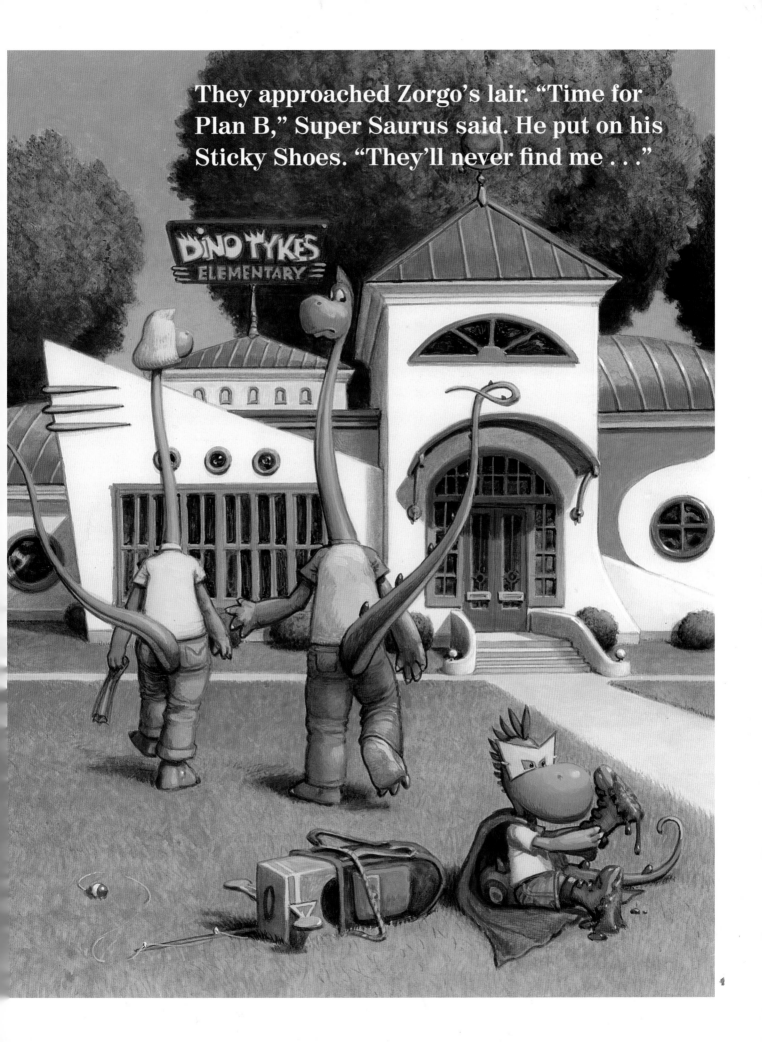

They approached Zorgo's lair. "Time for Plan B," Super Saurus said. He put on his Sticky Shoes. "They'll never find me . . ."

But Zorgo's spies were everywhere.

"Arnold, please," said Dad. "We don't want to be late on your first day."

A frightening figure loomed in the doorway.
ZORGO!

"Hi there! I'm Mr. Z," said Zorgo.

"I am Super Saurus."

"Okay, Super Saurus. Let's find your cubby," said Zorgo.

"See?" Emily whispered "No T. rex."

"Just wait," said Super Saurus.

"Good morning, everyone," said Zorgo.
"Please come to the carpet. It's song time!"

"Actually, I believe it's escape
time," muttered Super Saurus.

He hopped into his Super Saurus Rescue Rocket and zoomed off into a field of stars.

But then he heard howling.

His ship screeched to a halt. He couldn't leave all those innocent children in Zorgo's clutches!

There was only one thing to do.

Super Saurus narrowed his eyes. He straightened his mask. He marched up to Zorgo. "I challenge you to a duel!"

"We're singing right now," said Zorgo. "How about after snack time"

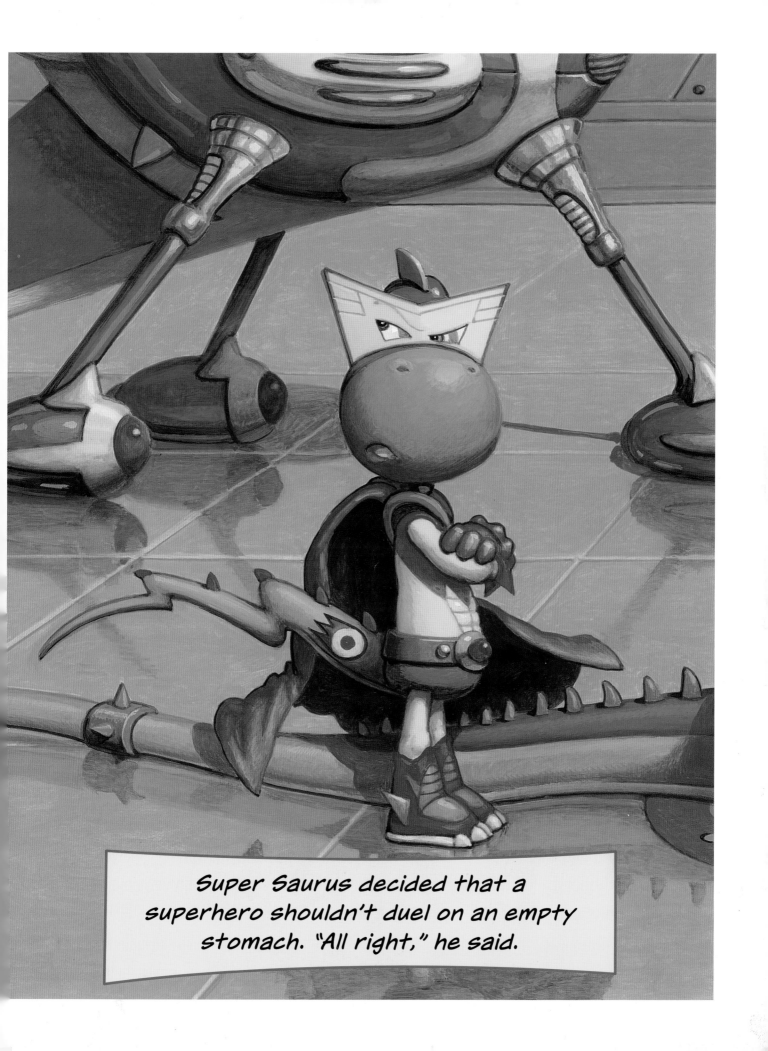

Super Saurus decided that a superhero shouldn't duel on an empty stomach. "All right," he said.

During art time, Super Saurus
painted signs for his hero hideout.

"Nice job,"
said Zorgo.

During free time, Super Saurus and Elmy made a villain trap out of Construct-O-Straws.

"Very creative!" said Zorgo.

During circle time, Super Saurus told how he conquered the Vacuum Viper.

"Wow—you are a superhero!" said Bosworth.

Finally, it was snack time. But just as Zorgo began to hand out raisins . . .

"I knew Zorgo couldn't be trusted!" cried Super Saurus.
"We don't eat snack. We ARE snack!"

"Don't worry, kids," said Zorgo. "We'll help him get out."

"Help him get out?" Super Saurus stared. "Isn't he going to eat us?"

"I think he'd rather have some raisins, don't you?" said Zorgo. "Come here, little guy."

"Wait! I have a plan!" said Super Saurus.

"Nice work, Super Saurus,"
said Emily.

"Can I be your sidekick?"
asked Bosworth.

When school was over, Mr. Z said good-bye.
"I'm sure glad you were here today, Super Saurus."

"Clearly kindergarten needs me," said Super Saurus.
"I'll be back tomorrow. And by the way..."

"... you can call me Arnold."

SUPER SAURUS!

a villain's worst nightmare —